Harry Meredith

Ranch 10

Annie from Massachusetts

Harry Meredith

Ranch 10
Annie from Massachusetts

ISBN/EAN: 9783337343187

Printed in Europe, USA, Canada, Australia, Japan

Cover: Foto ©Andreas Hilbeck / pixelio.de

More available books at **www.hansebooks.com**

Ranch 10.

OR

Annie from Massachusetts,

AN

AMERICAN MELODRAMA,

IN

Three Acts and Two Tableaux,

BY

HARRY MEREDITH.

Published by

T. SLATER SMITH,

AT THE OFFICE OF

"THE COURIER,"

No. 1107 Spring Garden Street.

Philadelphia.

CHARACTERS.

———

AL McCLELLAND. ⎞
TOM McCLELLAND. ⎠ Twin Brothers.

THEOPOLIS ROBBINS, M. D.

JOSEPH KEBOOK, Alias RED BULLET.

PETER PARTICULAR PROSE.

BARNEY HOLT.

PARSON JIM SCRIPTURE.

CORIANDER LUCRETIA SMALLEY.

ANNIE SMALLEY.

NEELY BARRETT.

SILVER BUD.

RANCH NO. 10.

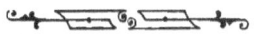

ACT I.

SCENE I.—*Exterior of Ranch.—Enter Bud, goes to feed birds. Enter Coriander, she takes down clothes from line and goes into house. Enter Neely, goes to wash tub, wrings out clothes, hangs them on line. Annie comes on, picks flower. All exit as soon as business is over. Cow-boy enters and goes into Ranch, one leaves Ranch and exits. Music through this until Kebook is on*

JOE. (*calling in house*)

JOE. I say, bring a me a pail of water for my a pony.

NEELY. [*at door*] So that's you Mr. Red Bullet is it? What do you want, a rope wid a noose in the end of it.

JOE. Bring a me a pail of water for my a pony.

NEELY. A pail of water is it well, well; there's a bucket in the house and water in the pump, help yourself or go wid out it.

JOE. Hiss! hiss! hiss! you no make a much a gab Miss Irish, bring a water for dat a pony and whiskey for de master.

NEELY. Water for both I should suggest, let the horse drink first and then the master dip his ugly head in the pail.

JOE. Hiss, hiss.

NEELY. Hiss away ye yellow snake.

JOE. Snake bite.

NEELY. Bah !

Enter CORIANDER.

CORI. What is all this fight about?

NEELY. I was only telling Red Bullet there, how much he looks like a basket of toads.

JOE. I want a my pony water.

CORI. Go and get the water for the poor beast.

NEELY. So I will ma-am, for your sake and the pony's, long life to him. [*she calls*] Joe ! Joe ! hiss ! hiss ! hiss !   [*Exit.*

JOE. I think a my money just as a good as anoders.

CORI. That's a matter of opinion. See here Mr. Red Bullet, Joe Kebook, I don't care ten foot of prairie land whether you'r as rich as men say you are, or as poor as little Silver Bud in the kitchen thar, it aint a man's roll of notes that makes him a king out here on the prairie, no sir! it's his inards, and if you have nothing better to recommend you to your fellow critters than your bank account down in Cheyene, the best thing you kin do in future is to pass right by Coriander L. Smalley and Ranch No. 10.   [*Exit.*

JOE. [*Seates himself.*] I don't get much a like here, men and woman a frown and a push, and make a swear at me; I wish I a dared to do it, there would be one more a grave in dat a prairie before Christmas. But if I should a kill dat Al McClelland even in fair fight, they would a hang a me to a telegraph pole before I could take my coat off. Hiss! hiss! [*up*] But Silver Bud, if I can a get her, oh, oh, good, good, dat a great news I love dat a gal dat a red squaw, if I can a get her, oh, dat a great news; but if I can't a get her—I dare not think of dat: [*Enter Silver Bud with pail*] See! see! stop a moment Bud, I've got a news, good a news, something from de fort for you, wait until I drink a my pony.

BUD. [*Going*] Me go now, Miss Cori wait.

JOE. [*Takes her down*] Let her wait, she made me wait a long enough; why can't you be a good a girl to me, Bud? See I have a brought you something to put in your little ears; gold hoops wid a spark in it.

BUD. No Joe, me no want spark, me afraid.

JOE. Come, a little squaw. [*He seizes her and kisses her passionately; she struggles and strikes him in the face.*]

JOE. You strike a me, hiss! hiss! if it wasn't for your pretty face, I choke you dead.

BUD. [*screams*] No, no, me no mean to.

JOE. Hush! talk like a whisper, some one may hear, gal I love you like mad; I love you like I hate a all other. Come Bud live with me. (*She starts to go*) Damma you shall. (*She struggles and breakes away, rushes up to steps, Joe seizes her about the waist, she pushes him desperately, and he falls. She exits.*)

JOE. (*After a pause*) Hiss, de only one in de world dat I don't hate, she strike a me, she spit at me, and she tread a me down like a snake: (*recovers*) Dare, no more, I am too a soft, I will do a work before night, big work. Freckle and dat gang come: good news, take a care No. 10. Red a Bullet is at work, my blood is boil. my heart is crack wid hate, hate! hiss! [*Exit.*

Enter ROBBINS. *meeting Joe. calling off.*

ROB. Oh no offence in the world, as the long buried William makes Hamlet say : I merely nodded to the horse and neglected you because I think the horse respectable, and you—well you are doubtful at all events. If Joe keeps on he will get himself talked about. House! I say, house! were it night I would exclaim : see what light through yonder window breaks! but as it is. I will content myself with remarking: that if my sense of smell can be depended on Miss Smalley has a delicious stew on the kitchen fire.   [*Music.*]

Enter ANNIE.

ANNIE. Good morning. Doctor. I'm afraid you have already put me on your sick report, as they say at the Fort; I'm quite bright to-day.

ROB. Bright! well I should say so; bright as a new nickle. How is your amiable relative?

ANNIE. Oh, Aunt is never sick you know.

ROB. Yes I know it to my sorrow; sick, no one gets sick here. (*Enter Cori.*) Good afternoon, Madame, in the language of a Rocky Mountain poet: the light of the burning sun flashes from your eyes, and the sound of a hundred cataracts burst from your lips.

CORI. That's a matter of opinion. Doctor; I want you to take care of this young lady by giving her as little of your compound extracts as possible; I brought her out here to give her a chance to breathe without swallowing New England fog every time she opened her mouth. I told her guardian that we were 7000 feet above Malaria. made no pies or sweet cakes, and that there was not a doctor within twenty miles—I forgot you when I made the statement.

ANNIE. Why Aunt, how can you!

ROB. Madame, in answer to your somewhat candid declaration. permit me to remark, that the time will come when you will be glad that my banishment has not been effectual; for should you happen to fall from your second story window and fracture your spinal column, for you have a spinal column, I shall be most happy to wait on your majestic person, and perform the delightful but delicate operation of carving you in two.

ANNIE. Is he offended Aunty?

CORI. Not he; we understand each other perfectly, as far as goodness in man goes he is tolerable, and as much as there is skill in doctors, he is bearable: now listen! Al McClelland is coming up the ravine; I saw him coming, with the glass five miles off.

ANNIE. Oh Aunty!

CORI. You unsophisteated little goose; I wish you were back in Massachusetts with your cough and bronchitis. The man's a picture I admit, but he's only a cow-boy, a good looking animal.

ANNIE. With a man's heart.

CORI. You poor deluded female woman, the old story—and so you are spoons on Al McClelland, hey!

ANNIE. I like him very much, Aunt.

CORI. Well, well, Chariots of Jerico! has he popped the question?

ANNIE. Yes Aunty, he has.

CORI. Dragons of Jerusalem! and you did'nt box his ears.

ANNIE. I could'nt Aunty, he held my hands so tight.

CORI. Well, I suppose there is no help for it; I wish it had been his brother Tom.

ANNIE. He has often spoken of Tom.

CORI. His twin brother—many a time I've had em mixed up when they were babies.

ANNIE. Exactly alike!

CORI. Alike, revelations of Melkesideck. Why their own dear mother used to have to guess at them often, and then give them up: now that they are men and the animals well grown, they are more like one another than ever; I have'nt seen Tom for ten years; I wish you had'nt seen his brother at all.

ANNIE. Be kind to us, Aunty?

CORI. Kind, well I'll hear what the fellow has to say—but I—I—I think you are real mean, Annie, to go away and—and—leave me. (*bursts into tears.*)

ANNIE. We won't go away Aunt.

CORI. Yes you shall, I won't have any of your dove and pigeon cooing about Ranch 10: why I could'nt cook the food, I could'nt eat my victuals; I'd walk in my sleep, fall into the rain-water hogshead, put poison in the batter-cakes, and end the whole affair by setting fire to the Ranch and burning you in your beds before the honey-moon was half over.

ANNIE. Oh what a tease you are!

CORI. Well have it your own way: now I must go into the house and bring these critters to order, men in the house and horses in the stable; men profane and the horses kick; the men would kick too if they dared; the horses are well enough in their way; but as for the men, I always wondered what they were sent into the world for.　　　　　　·　　　[*Exit both.*

　　　　　Enter JUDGE PROSE *and* HOLT.

PROSE. Well here we are at last! Ranch 10. This is the last until we reach the up river Ranches. Why is there no one here to receive me, I, a circuit Judge, as well as a government official: do they think a census taker is nobody?

HOLT. It looks like it.

PROSE. It's unambiguous, deleterious, infectuous, predestinationous; a delightful smell however comes from yonder kitchen, it's stupendous, futricious, meretricious, delicious.

HOLT. I'll tell you better after I've tasted it.

PROSE. You are altogether too irrational, irascible, detrimental, contemptimental. Is there any one alive in that house, if so, come forth and pay your respects to the representative of the grandest government under the sun; if you don't, I magnify you, bull doze you.

　　　　　　Enter CORIANDER.

CORI. That's a matter of opinion.

PROSE. Madame, why are we not waited on?

CORI. People generally wait on themselves here, and you can just bet your ears no one is going to jump over the moon because you have come.

PROSE. Do you know who I am *woman?*

CORI. No *man*, and don't want to know if you are no better than you look.

PROSE. Do you hear that, spurned like a wood-chuck by this prairie aligator; it's unacceptable, unalphabetical, diametrical— How many people have you in your house, woman?

CORI. They are in there eating; you kin go in and count em if you want to.

HOLT. Madame this is Judge Prose of the Cheyene Court.

appointed by the Government to take the census of this Territory, and I am his assistant.

CORI. [*shouts*] Oh, come to count the people have you, well what do you want of me?

PROSE. Madame, you had better reduce the number of words you use to the square inch, or may I be obliterated and extradited if you don't explode: call out your people. [*Takes out book.*

CORI. Annie come out here and git counted.

Enter ANNIE.

PROSE. Good evening Miss, I am taking the census.

CORI. Are you sure you have'nt taken leave of your senses.

PROSE. Repress yourself, slow down, break up, repose and capitulate: you stand in the presence of a Government Official: examine his height, take in the circumference of his waist-coat: do I fill the bill or not?

CORI. That's a matter of opinion.

PROSE. Holt, take down this irreverant woman's catagory. Now Miss, what is your name?

ANNIE. Annie Smalley.

PROSE. A quaint palpable name, not at all poetical or–or–or–

HOLT. Hysterical.

PROSE. No not hysterical, invulnerable: where were you born?

ANNIE. Rock River, Massachusetts.

PROSE. Rock River, indeed! most interesting: that's where the Pilgrim Fathers landed.

ANNIE. Oh no sir! that was Plymouth Rock.

PROSE. Hey! Plymouth—yes, yes, you are right. Plymouth Rock: have you any parents?

ANNIE. No Sir.

PROSE. How old are you?

CORI. Don't you tell him Annie.

ANNIE. Oh yes Aunty. Nineteen.

PROSE. They are always glad to tell their age when they are under twenty; who is next?

CORI. Annie, go and call Neely out. [*Annie goes up*] You kin count me while you are waiting for her.

PROSE. No, you'll keep until the last.

CORI. Why so.

PROSE. Because you are the toughest, and it will probably take all night to count you.

Enter NEELY and BUD.

CORI. You are a wretch.

PROSE. I am a Government Official.

CORI. Same thing.

PROSE. [*To Neely*] What are you called.

NEELY. Sure I'm called every morning at four o'clock.

PROSE. Your name?

NEELY. Neely Barrett from Tip.

PROSE. Tip! where's Tip?

NEELY. Oh sure he don't know where Tip is! Tip in Ireland.

PROSE. Ireland! where's Ireland?

NEELY. It's in Ireland now, one of these days it will be in the United States.

PROSE. How old are you?

NEELY. I'm purty well I thank you sir.

PROSE. Your age?

NEELY. [*runs to Annie*] How old are you, Miss Annie?

ANNIE. Nineteen.

NEELY. Sure, I'm nineteen sure.

PROSE. Well you look it.

CORI. Come here Bud.   [*Bud goes down* L.

PROSE. In the name of the great jumping Giraffe! where did you catch that? You murderous looking red-skin! what is your name?

BUD. Silver Bud.

PROSE. How many scalps have you hanging in your wigwam?

BUD. Me no scalp, Great Spirit say bad; me love, me sing, me kiss.

PROSE. Remarkable young savage! spends her time kissing and singing. Daughter of Sitting Bull approach, come hither Pocahantas, Silver Bud. The pale-faced official of a mighty nation stretches forth his arm to patronize you. Minnehaha be patronized. Holt, make a note of this little incident; it's amiacable, susceptible, allegorical. Now Madame, I'm ready for you.

CORI. Coriander Lucretia Smalley, born in Massachusetts; had the small-pox twice, never been vacinated, good bodily health; real estate owner; never been married thank heaven!

PROSE. Feeling better now?

CORI. I always feel tolerably well.

PROSE. How old are you?

CORI. That's my business.

PROSE. Put her down sixty-eight.

CORI. He shant! I'm only forty-two.

PROSE. Forty-two, I thought I'd fetch you. Who else have you here permanently.

CORI. No one else: cow-boys coming and going all the time.

ANNIE. Oh yes Aunty! Al, you know.

CORI. Al McClelland, he is not a resident here, and I hope it will be a long time before he is.

PROSE. Who is this Al McClelland? I've heard of him in Cheyene; Dandy Al they call him, a turbulent fellow always fighting; why only a month ago he thrashed a desperado, Portugee Joe, within an inch of his life—and—

ANNIE. Stop sir! I must correct you when you speak ill of Al McClelland. I know the truth regarding the circumstance of which you speak; Joseph Kebook is the owner of a number of wretched tenements in Cheyene, from one of these a Sheriff's officer was expelling a poor family. Kebook was assisting in his brutal way, and was using unnecessary force against a young girl, a cripple, who could not move as quickle as the rest; he pushed her roughly and the poor child fell to the ground. McClelland was passing and saw it all; in the glory of his manhood he fell upon the pitiable monster, and punished him as the lion would the coward wolf; this is the man whose character you would blacken; this is the man of whom I would say to you, go and do likewise.

PROSE. Holt, I've very important business ten miles from here. Madame, show us the way to your bar; I'll liquor up, jump into my gig, and get as far away from your Ranch as possible, I think I'm a match for any one woman in the world, but when it comes to four, I'd rather be keel-dragged through a hundred Volcanoes, or face a dozen Earth-quakes. Madame, I take my official departure prematurely, substantially, argumentalisely, spermatically.   [*Exit with Holt.*

· CORI. Government official! well if they are all like him, it's no wonder the government has to pay a hundred-thousand-dollars a year for carrying an empty mail bag ten miles.

                                      [*Exit* CORI. BUD. NEELY.

ANNIE. Around me all nature smiles, and with this blessed

warmth comes to my soul a glorious flood of happiness. He is coming to me now, swift as the wind that chases his pony across the prairie; I trust, I believe him; he is my own.

Enter AL.

AL. Forever little Starbell! why those are not eyes, they are prairie flames growing right out of your forehead.

ANNIE. Oh Al, I am so safe now; so happy, so glad, are you glad too.

AL. Glad, why Annie that is a poor name for it; have you yet given a hint of our little secret to the amiable guardian of your health and conscience?

ANNIE. Yes, and I think that in the end we will find a warm champion in Aunt Cori.

AL. Aunt Cori is a brick ! I suppose she gave me a terrible turning over, did'nt she?

ANNIE. Oh yes indeed ! and she said she wished it was your brother Tom who was in love with me.

AL. Indeed ! dear old Tom; well you might do worse Annie, don't be shocked when you meet him Annie, Tom has never enjoyed the advantages given to brother Phil and I; he is rough in speech, in manner most positive, but his heart is as big as his body, and he's worth a dozen such fellows as I am.

ANNIE. He is then very like you.

AL. We are one and the same, bless his dear face; my noble twin brother ! But Annie when he comes here don't you ever mistake him for me.

ANNIE. Is he coming then ?

AL. Yes, I took the liberty of anticipating Miss Cori's consent and wrote to Tom that it was all right, and that he was to come at once and see his brother take the fearful leap. Tom has at length put his pick into a streak of silver that assays very lively. He is in Colorado, his claim is at Wild Cry Gulch, in Silver Creek Cannion.

ANNIE. Bless him, and bless you dear Al, and now not another word of nonsense until I have paid some attention to that awful appetite of yours.

AL. It's worse than ever Annie; a slice of antelope, a couple of snowy rolls, and a bowl of milk will put me in marching order and enable me to assault that formidable fortress, Coriander L. Smalley.

ANNIE. She will soon surrender.

AL. She had better, or I will storm the outworks, take the citadel and carry off the prize by force of arms—come little one and see the performance.   [*Exit Al.*

ANNIE. He does love me, and I love him with all my trusting heart, with all the love that heaven has planted in my soul; why then, should I see sorrow in the future; what cloud is it that seems to rise between us to-night? He is near me, why am I not as happy as I hoped to be? There is one thing I can do, trust to God as truly as I trust him.   [*Song and Exit.*

Chorus.]   Enter TOM MCCLELLAND, *stands until chorus is over.*

TOM. That's a mournful kind of a tune. My brother Al writ to me to come yhar to a wedding; it sounds more like a funeral. Thar's a tidy lump of a woman; wonder if that aint Annie—brother Al's Annie; this is the place sure enough; Ranch 10. Wonder if Al's yhar yit? They must be feeding in thar from the sound of the knives and forks. I wont speak a word to a· soul until I've swept up my claim a bit, and shook some of the gold and silver dust out of my beard, then I'll jump out on Annie and Al like a Jack Rabbit, and hug em like a Grizzly Bar. Thars a sleeping room, 16, 17, 18; 18, I'll go right in thar—hello! who's thar?

Enter ROBBINS *looking at Tom.*

ROB. Good Evening, McClelland.

TOM. That's my name Stranger, whar did you git on to it?

ROB. [*looking at him*] Come here Me, I want your advise about those cattle I bought.

·TOM. Stranger, I arnt over particular; but as sure as nuggets is gold, I don't intend to speak a word to a soul in this yhar dead level grass county until I have rested two hours, cleaned my guns and put my bosom outside of five pound of Antelope meat; no disrespect stranger, but the man who always looks behind him, never gits shot in the back. [*goes into* 18.]

ROB. Al McClelland come back ! Is the man drunk or mad? How strangely he speaks, one of his jokes I suppose; he has shut himself up in 18 room, he called me stranger. [*Goes to door and shakes it.*] All right Mr. McClelland, the next time you come to me with a cattle punchers knife in your ribs, maybe I wont sew up the wound with a wax-end and a shoemaker's needle.

Enter AL. McCLELLAND.

AL. All right Annie, thank you. Oh, Doctor! good evening: my supper aint quite ready yet. Annie's going to prepare it herself; that's enough to make a fellow eat. I've come out to have a crack at some of those hawks that get away with Miss Smalley's chickens.

ROB. Well upon my word! jumped out of the window, did you? Little more civil now, with your yhar and your thar, and your stranger; all right stranger, the man who always looks behind him never gits shot in the back. [*Exit.*

AL. Is the man drunk or mad? There's that cold blooded snake Red Bullet, picketing his pony; I suppose he's going to stay here to-night; how I'd like to let both pannels go at him, and disfigure his clothes between the shoulders; well I have'nt come to shooting people in the back, though I believe Joe will do it for me if he ever gets the drop.

SILVER BUD *comes down and throws her arms about Al.*

AL. Now Bud no more of that; it wont do. [*she weeps*] there, little indian don't cry, its no use, you know I've told you so before.

BUD. Oh Al! me love much, me love better than Miss Annie; let me love little bit.

AL. I have never given you cause for this, poor child, you promised me you would'nt speak of this again, Silevr Bud.

BUD. Yes but now you go away, and marry Miss Annie, me never see you no much, no more.

AL. [*loudly*] Now this must stop; hush! here's your mistress.

Enter CORIANDER.

CORI. What are you scolding that poor girl about? Look out Al McClelland, I loved your dear dead mother long ago, and for her sake I loved her twin sons Tom and Al, but if you illtreat this helpless child, you shall never again see as much as an old hair-pin that belongs to my niece Annie Smalley.

AL. I am not in the habit of ill-treating women, Miss Smalley.

CORI. Oh I never trusted one of you; if I had, I might have been dragged into some terrible matrimonial infelicity myself. [*Exit.*

BUD. Al me promise be good girl, let Bud go too; me scrub, me wash, me cook, me sing all the time; let little injun go too.

AL. By the fires of unquenchable forked lightning, you shall go, and never want for a home while the principal member of the McClelland family has got a slab of lumber over his head. [*she kisses his hand and weeps*] There little Bud, don't.   [*aside* Poor little thing.   Bud, do you see that hawk sailing over the prairie in the moonlight? I'll bring you the feathers from that bird to make a fan for your mistress; the little squaw has broken me all to pieces; if I don't shoot the feathers out of that bird's tail pretty soon, I'll have a fit.   [*Exit.*

    JOE *has been watching Scene up stage, now he comes down and touches Bud on shoulder.*]

JOE. Bud !

BUD. [*turns in terror*] No go.

JOE. Will you go with a me ?

BUD. No, me stay.

JOE. You love dat Al.

BUD. Yes me love—you me hate.

JOE. You hate !

BUD. Yes.

JOE. Damn !

BUD. Go !   [*Picture. He moves slowly away and goes off* R. to E.   *Bud turns to* L. I. E.

BUD. Yes Al, Bud always love; but no say, but only cry a little bit in bed; dear Al ! maybe me cry all the time. [*Shot heard off* R. U. E. *and* L. U. E.   BUD *falls* C.   Al love Bud now, poor Bud sick; in good land; Bud love all time, Al, Al, Bud sick, Bud glad. [*Gasps and dies* C.

    Enter AL MCCLELLAND, L. I. E.   *Murmurs in house.*

AL. I'll give that gun away to the first blind man I meet; I can't hit a hawk in the bright moonlight; a bird as big as a pony—never mind Bud I'll— [*spring over to the body*] Why Bud ! what is it girl? If you have got breath enough to speak, let me hear you.   Blood ! the girl is dead ! [*hurried rush of people from the house.   Enter* CORI., ROB., NEELY *and* ANNIE.   JOE *and his gang enter from* R. U. E. *All down.*

CORI. Who fired that shot? What's this? Bud ! McClelland !

ANNIE. Speak Al !

AL. Hush, hush, all ! we are here with the dead !

ALL Dead ?

AL. Don't you see the poor little toad all shot to rags, the blood streaming out of her and melting into the dry prairie?

CORI. Poor little one!

ANNIE. Poor little Silver!

ROB. Ladies stand up, and Al McClelland, straighten yourself like a man that I know you to be, and tell us who did this.

AL. Did it! by the Lord that made me, I'd give my arm to the shoulder to know the coward who did it. I would'nt kill him with a single rip of my knife, but I'd tear his limbs from his body, and then drop him out on the prairie for the wolves to play with. This poor little homeless girl has gone indeed: I'd give half my heart's blood to bring her back! that wont do it; but I'll give a hundred head of cattle for the name of the coward who did this work.

JOE. [rushes down] I claim dat hundred cattle.

ROB. You know the man?

JOE. Yes.

ALL Who?

JOE. Al McClelland.

AL jumps for him. Robbins throws him over L.

ROB. Keep quiet man! leave this to me.

AL. My God! me!

ROB. Hold up your head and look the man you accuse in the face.

AL. He can't do it! if he can, I'll own I did it.

JOE. She was his a gal, he wanted to get a rid of her.

AL. You lie! you snake.

ROB. Go on Joe.

JOE. I heard a loud words between them.

CORI. Good heavens! they were quarrelling.

AL gets up stage.

JOE. By and by him raise dat a gun and fire.

CORI. We heard the shot: oh horrible!

JOE. [picks up gun] One barrel empty, and look! see blood on his hand.

AL. I can't think. I can hardly see. Oh God above, make me blind if you will, but don't curse me with madness! Annie.

ANNIE. Here Al.

AL. Do you believe?

ANNIE. Innocent.

JOE. Me do not. Take and hang quick! [all start for Al.

AL. [draws pistols] Back! you've tried to steal my honor.

now come and try to take my life. Red Bullet I did not kill that girl, and you know that I did not; I don't mean to be hung up in the moonlight by you or your gang of train-wrecking horse thieves, so look out for the moment, when backed by the rifles of honest men, I stand ready to fasten this devilish sin on the head of the coward to whom it belongs.   [*Rushes up and slams door. The mob rush up break open. Then they all fall back as* CORI. *rushes through them, she goes to door of* 18 *room, shakes the knob.*

CORI. This door is locked; McClelland come out.   [*she goes down.* ANNIE *is on her knees.*]   Annie hold up your aching head and bring your broken heart to me. [ANNIE *runs to* CORI. I believe in your lover's truth, but the world wont; he must defend himself here. (*to the men*) He is in 18 room, break the door open.   [JOE *goes up and breaks in door.* TOM *appears and comes down. All stand in picture. He stumbles over body.*

TOM. What's hyar? Is this the way you do in this dead level grass country? Butcher little squaws and then put em under people's feet for em to stumble over. What do you mean by waking a man out of his sound sleep by chopping his door into fire-wood?

ROB. Al McClelland, have you gone clean crazy?

ANNIE. [*rushes to him*] Al, Al, Al!

TOM. (*aside*) Al McClelland, Al! (*siezes her*) Come hyar Miss quick! (*takes her down*)

JOE. Now grab him tight!   (*they start*)

ROB. Stand off! let the man have a chance; he's talking to a lady now; and the first cow-puncher that interrupts that heart-broken woman, I'll make a fit subject for a dissecting room; get back!   (*they go up stage*)

ANNIE. Oh Al! what will become of us?

TOM. Hush! look again Miss.   (ANNIE *utters a half stiffled scream*) Hush! your woman's heart tells you what yhar eyes did not; you called me Al jist now—you are Annie.

ANNIE. Yes, and you are brother Tom.

TOM. Yes I am brother Tom; I came hyar to your wedding, because Al writ to me to come quick; I went in thar to rest—I war asleep on the bed when they bust the door open—but tell me quick, what of brother Al?

ANNIE. This poor girl has been murdered and they——

TOM. They accuse him, my brother Al! they lie, they lie, they lie! but quick! what of Al?

ANNIE. Gone—fled through the house.

TOM. Fled! my soul! and they take me for him.

ANNIE. Yes, and he will soon be beyond the reach of danger.

TOM. Now look me in the face. Did Al McClelland do this yhar?

ANNIE. No! no! no!

TOM. God bless you sis, I knowed it; and you love him dear, don't you?

ANNIE. Better than my life.

TOM. Thar it's all over, cheer up little one, I swar in the name of the good man above, not to desart you or brother Al.

ANNIE. What are you going to do?

TOM. Hush! Tom McClelland has dropped out of the light of man praps forever, and yhar in his place stands Al the man accused.

ANNIE. No, a 'single word will save you.

TOM. No gal, this yhar aint my work or yourn; it is the work of him who stamped the same image on us two boys—remember it's his claim we are working.　[*Annie goes up, Tom turns to Joe.*] Gentlemen, I aint going to defend myself with words.

JOE. Now grab.　(*Robbins interferes.*)

TOM. Stop! for I swar in the name of the man that made them stars, there shall be no fighting about me while we are standing hyar with our feet in the blood of this dead indian; I surrender myself to be tried by the laws of God and man, and if thars a warm spot in your souls an inch square, you'll feel for the poor devil, who stands yhar accused of this awful crime: and of which he swars in the name of the great Jehovah, he is innocent.

JOE. You talk too much, hang!

ANNIE. (*screams*) No! no,! hear me! he is not—

TOM. (*seizing her*) Annie what do you mean! do not speak.

ANNIE. I must speak; justice first—love afterwards.

ALL Speak!

ANNIE. He is not——

TOM. (*seizes her and buries her face in his bosom*) He is not guilty: that's what she would say. Gentleman, he is not guilty!

CURTAIN.

ACT II.

SCENE II.—*Interior of Corrall, boxing stockade, hut across stage, in 3 large folding doors. Gate* L. *down by one. Cow-boy asleep at table with musket, fire of sticks* L.

Enter ROBBINS *at gate, goes and shakes Sentry.*

ROB. Wake up! you lazy, snoring, sleepy wolf; keep your eyes open, and your mouth shut, or I'll be ham strung and quartered if you don't swallow that musket; to say nothing of loosing your prisoner. Get outside and don't you go to sleep again. [*Cow-boy exits*] Sleep that knits up the ravelled sleeve of care; if a fellow could only sleep long enough he might get his entire wardrobe repaired. Good evening madame, are you feeling as well as you look?

CORI. That's a matter of opinion; there's another pesky dis. turbance about McClelland, dear oh dear! I've scolded until my head aches.

ROB. [*taking her hand*] Who has dared to give you a heart-ache—I mean a head-ache.

CORI. That little sawed off Judge from Cheyene is here; the one that counted me and the girls; he has been storming like a blizzard, and says that I ought not to have allowed McClelland to be kept here.

ROB. Oh well, his judicial majesty need give himself no further concern. Sheriff McDow in Cheyene, deputized Joe Kebook to take charge of the prisoner, and he is legally detained. Now I have used my somewhat versatile powers of persuasion, and McDow has cut off Kebook's head and appointed me sole guardian of Mr. Al McClelland.

CORI. Well you are a good little round critter after all; is the poor boy to be kept in there until the trial?

ROB. No, he will, at all events, be as much in the hands of the law, out on the prairie; as in there, these drunken cow-boys drawing pay from Kebook, as his guards, carouse all day, and sleep on post at night; if he had chosen, he could have escaped a dozen times; to-morrow I'm going to clear him out of this, take his word that he will appear for trial at Cheyene, and allow him the freedom that I am sure, rightly belongs to him—and that's my opinion of Mr. Al McClelland.

CORI. Why, you are really worth something after all, you have made my head feel better already.

ROB. [*takes her hand*] Don't neglect to call on me if you have a relapse, my remedies are very simple, and I shall always be most happy to prescribe; [*strokes her hand*] feeling quite well now?

CORI. [*turns away smiling*] That's a matter of opinion.

Enter NEELY with tray.

ROB. Decidedly! oh, here comes the fair mistress of the larder, with smoking provocations to appetite. What have you there, Miss Delmonico?

NEELY. Sure I have a good supper for a good man; the fellow that can eat the way he does, never had the heart to murder poor Bud.

ROB. And the man that can swear like that at seven P. M. must have plenty of conscience, and that conscience made of excellent material.

CORI. Aint that unfortunate animal had his roasted hen yet? [*Looks in centre doors and screams*]

ROB. What is the commotion?

NEELY. What is it ma-am?

CORI. The wretch is on the bed!

ROB. I hope he is'nt under the bed.

NEELY. People do go to bed sometimes, ma-am.

CORI. That's a matter of opinion.

TOM. (*inside*) Who's out thar?

ROB. Three charming ladies; a distinguished medical practioner; half a broiled chicken, six eggs, with the usual surrounding, the last named are rapidly cooling off.

Enter TOM.

TOM. I'll warm em. Evening ladies; I warn't asleep ma-am, I jist lay down thar rough shod like an army hoss, and I got a thinking— [*sees ANNIE enter, crosses to her.*] Good evening sis, is your heart brave?

ANNIE. I'm trying hard, Tom.

TOM. Keep your soul warm child, mine is, mine is. [*goes to table*] Thank you ladies: Doctor, when a man kin eat like this yhar, he aint no need of your sarvices.

CORI. That's a matter of opinion; some of your sex would

eat perched up on a red hot stove, and sleep on the top of a lightning rod.

ROB. Right. ma-am, I was once amputating a leg—(*she starts*) a gentleman's leg; when I began to carve, he took down his fiddle and began to play, would you believe it ma-am ! before I had the bone half sawed through, the fellow was fast asleep with the fiddle under his head for a pillow.

CORI. That's a matter of opinion.

ROB. Well perhaps this is rather breezy kind of chaff for Mc-Clelland to be obliged to swallow with his supper and his trouble; let's leave him to his evening work.

CORI. Tell him first that to-morrow he is no longer to be shut up in this crazy old buffalo pen.

ROB. (*goes behind table*) Al old fellow, (*he starts*) I've got a good piece of inteligence to read right into your ear: you are now my prisoner, I am your sheriff; at sun-rise to-morrow, you shall walk out of that gate and go where you please until your trial takes place—will you pledge me your word to appear at the Cheyene Court when we want you ?

TOM. (*in sad wonder*) Going to send me away from yhar ?

CORI. Precepts of Israel ! why the man looks as if he was going to be lynched !

TOM. (*looks at Annie*) No ma-am, but I aint got no other place to go in the wide world but yhar.

ROB. What do you mean ? Go up to your Ranch at Stemmers, and live there until we need you.

CORI. No place to go ! why the man has more friends than any one in the territory.

TOM. (*aside looking at Annie*) Friends, what are friends to me now— (*recovers*) Thar, I'm getting to be a kid; thank you Robbins, do with me as you like; yes, I promise, thanks; bless you all. [CORI. *takes his left hand,* ROBBINS *his right.* NEELY *pats him on the back,* ANNIE *goes into shed.*

ROB. Now then let's leave him to his repast; by the way ma-am, speaking of eating, what shall we enjoy for breakfast.

CORI. That's not a matter of opinion.

ROB. Not much information derived from that witness, Neely; Miss Neely, was'nt that a string of prairie fowl I saw hanging up in the bar ?

NEELY. Yes, wont they make a fine roast Doctor ?

Rob. Roast doctor, oh I see; yes, delicious.

Neely. Fat.

Rob. Yes.

Neely. Tinder.

Rob. Yes.

Neely. Young.

Rob. Oh rapture! there must be a couple of dozen.

Neely. Yis, a couple of dozen.

Rob. Are they for breakfast?

Neely. That's not a matter of opinion.   [*Exit.*

Rob. That girl was trying to pump me; I will leave that unfortunate man under charge of Kebook's guards, for the last time to-night; to-morrow there will be a dozen bold spirits up from Cheyene, and some officers from the fort; then if the Kebook gang assert their authority, I will produce my official documents and, aided by my saintly confederates, will use upon their horse stealing bodies, certain powerful remedies not classified in any erudite volume of Medical Science.   [*Exit.*

    Annie *comes from shed and touches Tom.*

Tom. [*timidly*] Annie, sis, you thar, what were you doing in thar?

Annie. Trying to tidy your room a bit, Tom.

Tom. You do that for me, no sis, not with them white hands.

Annie. Yes Tom, for you just as I would for Al; do you know Tom that at times, you are both as one to me— Tom and Al and Annie all one.

Tom. And little brother Phil out in Omaha, don't forgit bud.

Annie. Strange, I feel it here Tom, what is going to happen? Oh this awful future!

Tom. We'll meet it all together Annie, not even death shall seperate us boys and you; kin you guess where the dear one is now?

Annie. Oh, that I could!

Tom. Why did'nt he never used to talk to you with tears in his eyes, of brother Tom down in old Colly? Did'nt he used to tell you that down thar war the dearest and best pardner he ever owned in the world?

Annie. Yes, yes.

Tom. Well then little one, when this yhar trouble blast came unto him like starvation on a winter prairie, or death down in a flooded mine, whar should he go but to Tom, down to the peak—down to the centre of the Rockies.

ANNIE. [*springs up*] Gone to your claim in Colorado !

TOM. True again, sis; like the bird that went back to the good man in the scripture book; so he went for Tom because Tom war his great ark of safety.

ANNIE. (*down*) And there I will follow him.

TOM. You ! no, no Annie you could never make it; it's a hundred miles away from any rail road; no woman has ever been thar yit.

ANNIE. Then I shall not go as a woman; in the garments of your sex; with a man's heart and a woman's love in that heart I will go.

TOM. No ! no ! I cannot let you go.

ANNIE. Why Tom, is it not my duty ?

TOM. (*aside*) This child teaches me my duty. Sister Annie, from the time I war a boy at home with brother Al, before little Phil were born, I aint never said one single prayer; but sister Annie, if I know what prayin is, I'm a praying now, I'm a prayin now.

ANNIE. Amen, and so am I. [*Song by Annie*] Tom, dear Tom, be brave still dear brother. I will go and find Al, tell him all, and bring him back to right this wrong, or at least get from him, some clue that will fasten the guilt where it belongs.

TOM. (*aside*) I must hold out ! no more, or I am wus than a cur dog. You shall go. When ?

ANNIE. To-night I can get everything ready at once.

TOM. Fifty miles west of Greely is the town of Cold Claim, thar, lives Parson Jim Scripture——

CORI. (*inside*) Don't you dare to stop me !

TOM. Hush ! hyar is your Aunty.

Enter CORI.

ANNIE. I was just coming to you Aunty.

CORI. Thats a matter of opinion; Niece, thars a bigger feeling in my heart for that man than I choose to tell either you or him; first, I don't believe he is a cut-throat in spite of the proof that may yet break his neck; no man with Abby McClelland's blood warming his heart, could do a cowardly murder.

TOM. Bless you, ma-am.

CORI. More still he loves you; but all the same, he aint no fit

companion for you, nor is this the place for a young girl, about
whom half the cow-boys in No. 10 begin to whisper and wonder.

ANNIE. Oh Aunty!

TOM. Stop ma-am.

CORI. It's my speech, man! and you might as well try to dip
up Niagara Falls with a yankee pail as to shut me up when I've
got something to say; Al McClelland, you don't need to have
no new charge laid again you; don't meet this girl alone again,
until the law has said, thar is nothing red on your hand.

Annie, you have been given into my keep by them that loves
you and trusts me; I don't believe there's an ill drop of blood
under your skin, but when a lot of mean, cowardly, sneaking
men begin to hint and wink, it's time for some elderly female,
about my size, to roll up her sleeves and see that no lies are
told about the orphan girl living under her roof; and that's my
opinon first, last, all the time, and twice on Sunday.   [Exit.

TOM. Yes, she must go; to keep her hyar longer, would be a
sin; to keep her hyar would bring a hunger into my heart that
would make me hate myself and cuss my brother Al; I'd die
joyful to see her his wife to-day; I'd be willing then to say one
more prayer, hyar one more song from her lips, and then go
right out to the boys, say, gentlemen I done it, and die in my
boots. Oh! I'm in a heap of trouble sar, for myself and them I
car for; I hope the good man will keep my soul warm, for it
needs warming.

JOE. [outside] I am Deputy Sheriff in charge of that a prisoner. [enters] Good a morning, Al.   •

TOM. [busy with chair] I'm looking towards you, sar.

JOE. Well, Al McClelland, I have a got de drop on a you dis
a time, and it will a be a cold a day if I don't a get dare now.

TOM. I'm listening to you, sar, go on.

JOE. I'm getting a back at you now for dat a time you knock
a me under de billiard table in Cheyene; oh! I'm glad I did'nt
shoot a you den, for I'm a getting back for de red a gal you
stole from me.

TOM. I'm listening to you, sar, go on.

JOE. I often get a hungry and a parch to get a back at your a
carcass, but I never know how until you tumble right under
my feet, and I could so easy put the blood of dat a gal on you.

TOM. Then it war you who put her blood on me?

JOE. Who says so, not I?

TOM. I'm listening to you, sar, go on.

JOE. I heard you talk to Bud dat a night, I heard her a beg for your love; I heard you shut dat a gal's mouth, and tell her dat you take her up de river, for servant of dat a green and yellow Yankee gal you going to marry.

TOM. (*springs at him*) You damned Cayotte! [*Joe raises gun. Tom puts up his hands*]

JOE. You look a wild now, and keep a still.   [*he gets excited and forgetful*] I always knew she love a you, but when I see her squeeze a your hand and beg for your love, my blood tremble and boil up.

TOM. (*eagerly*) I'm listening to you, sar, go on.

JOE. (*madly*) Den I saw my chance; you ran away to shoot dat hawk. I come to beg once more for dat a gal to love a me; she spit on me, and slap a me, hate! hiss! I get a wild, crazy. I raised dat a gun—

TOM. And fired!

JOE. (*recovering*) No. no, I ran away!

TOM. You lie, you raised your gun and killed Silver Bud!

JOE. Dat a lie!

TOM. True! the words were jumping right out of your mouth her blood is shining right in your eye, see! thar she is behind you.   [*Joe utters a cry of fright, turns quickly, drops gun. Tom stands on it*] I'm listening to you, sar, go on. Not guilty! I I knowed it; oh Al boy, forgive me if I doubted you for a moment. [*puts Joe's gun away.*] You unclean warmint, that hes crawled into day-light; you cowardly snake, that bites behind and then runs away; I've got a little brother Phil out in Omaha; if that thar kid war hyar, I'd make him beat out your brains with his slate and pencil; but as he aint hyar– [*struggle and fall.* PAT STRANGLE *appears on stockade with gun, aims at Tom who is over Joe.*]

PAT. Drop that man, and hold up your hands. *Tom holds up his hands and Pat lowers gun. Tom seizes pistols from Joe's belt and aims at Pat.*

TOM. Drop that thar gun, and hold up your hands! (*Pat does so.   After applause,* ROBBINS *bursts through the gate, rushes for Tom and takes the pistols away from him.*

TOM. Robbins, this hyar fiend has jist confessed that he murdered Silver Bud the injun gal, I dragged it from him word by word; look at him as he lies thar, and judge between him and me; am I a liar or he a red stained murderer?

ROB. Well I for one am not indisposed to believe you, but there is no law in medical science, I mean in legal practice, that can convict a man on his own confession, given away from the hearing of disinterested witnesses. I should advise you to let the deputy Sheriff up before you pump all the wind out of him with your boots. [*Joe rises*]

JOE. Hate! hiss! in one week from to-day—

ROB. (*throws him around*) See here Red Bullet, if you or your congregation there interfere with this man's comfort, to the limited extent of causing him to drop an eyelash to the ground. I'll perform an operation on your anatomy not set down in any erudite volume of Medical Science.

JOE. I am Deputy Sheriff in charge of dat a man.

ROB. You were genial Joe, but your official career exists only in the past tense; your successor is already on the ground.

JOE. Who?

ROB. Theopolis Robbins M. D.

JOE. Hiss!

ROB. Hiss away, Joe, it pleases you and we don't mind; here is sheriff McDow's warrant and here is your high bounce. [*hands Joe paper*] For to-night this man is the sole owner of the enclosed premises; to-morrow he shall go where it strikes him he will do the most good; and if any of you doubt my authority, in the language of that good old gentleman from Tenn. I take the responsibility—crawl out.　　　　[*Exit outlaws.*]

JOE. [*gets his gun and crosses, turns at gate*] Hiss!

ROB. This caucus is disolved.　　　　[*Exit JOE.*]

TOM. Pardner they dug you out of a good piece of rock—free gold; hold on to this a moment.　　　　(*they clasp hands*)

ROB. No need to tell you to keep your tongue still; to-morrow some of my following are to gallop over from Cheyene, then you may depart as you please, until you are wanted by old Judge Prose in Cheyene. Above all things, respect the feelings of these poor people whose hospitality you enjoy; don't let any of these rounders connect your name with Annie Smalley as they did with Silver Bud.

TOM. Hold on man!

ROB. There I am speaking for the good of all; don't see her again until your good name is established.

TOM. I wont! bless her, I wont!

ROB. I will send you a green glass bottle containing a mixture both cheering, stimulating and exhilarting; the contents of which, however delightful to us, is not of sufficient significance to bear frequent mention in any erudite volume of Medcal Science.   [*Exit.*

TOM. And now the time is come for Annie and I to part forever, the only one who knows that I am not Al McClelland, is going off to life and happiness.   She kin save me before she goes: she must speak.   But I have sworn to save her lover, my brother Al; I have sworn to stay and suffer in his place; if I break that oath and he is took again, it will be sartain death for her as well as him.   I'll not break either word or oath; jump on your pony brave girl and go for the man you love, I'll stay right hyar and trust to my great big North American luck to save my neck.   [*Exit into shed.*

Enter ANNIE *under-dressed as a boy.*

AN. The sentinel is asleep at his post; I trembled as I passed him; I am certain I saw something crouching in the grass directly in my path, a wild beast or still worse, some of Kebook's spying accomplices; a word with my noble Tom and then begins the fight.   (*knocks at shed*)

TOM. [*at door*] Annie, sis, you hyar? No! no! quick then! Parson Jim Scripture at Cold Claim, is the man you want to go for; don't try to deceive him about anything; in the name of a helpless woman, kindly beg that good man to lead you to the Western Belle and put you safe in the arms of my brother Al; is your pony ready?

ANNIE. Yes. saddled and picketed down in the ravine; you see Tom, I have begun to work for myself.   [*Joe appears and darts off again*]

TOM. What was that? Some one at that thar gate; Annie, I tremble for your good name; not for my life would I have you found hyar now. [*goes and fastens gate*] Are you strong Annie?

ANNIE. Yes Tom, let me hold your hand for a moment.

TOM. (*takes her hand*) Don't you tremble child, when you find my brother Al, don't wait for food or drink, but drag him down on his knees before Jim Scripture, and make the good old feller speak the words that gives you to him forever—oh. Annie! until that is done, don't you never look upon my face again, not even to speak the words that would save me from the gallows.

ANNIE. (*eagerly*) Oh Tom, why?

TOM. Because I—I— (*aside*) Because my poor sore heart would break through my bosom, and she would see all that thar is writ upon it.— Don't tell Al that I am hyar keeping watch for him, he'd come flying back like some great eagel to pull Tom out of danger.

ANNIE. But Tom you must be saved, and these terrible men in Kebook's employ, will come perhaps and put you to a disagreeable death.

TOM. Annie, Kebook killed Silver Bud; in his mad rage to-day I pulled the words right out of his mouth; we have no proof, but that man fears me, and I have got ready for him long ago. In that old store shed amongst other things, I found a part of a keg of powder; that powder I have planted under that old building and under that stockade; that fire burns thar night and day; if the wust comes to wust, and them fellows attempt to take the law in their own hands, I'll blow em up to the clouds, as I am a living man, I will! And now Annie, it is time for you to go. [*sho' fired*] What is that?

ANNIE. The alarm at the Ranch, they are after me! Tom, what shall I do? [*shouts outside*]

TOM. In! in, quick! (*he puts her in shed, locks door*)

ROB. (*outside*) Open the door or I will break it down with a wagon pole!

CORI. Open the gate!

TOM *runs and opens gate, all rush on.*

CORI. Where is she, scoundrel?

TOM. Thar is no scoundrel hyar ma-am.

ROB. (*with knife*) Is Miss Smalley here McClelland? If she is it's death for you or I; if she is not it's the work of a coward and a liar.

TOM. (*up to him*) Hold on man!

JOE. She is in that hut.

CORI. Search it! [*All start for door*]

TOM. Stop, you shall not! thar's an oak door and six feet of good solid man to go through, before you kin enter that thar room.

ROB. McClelland, when I touched your hand to-day, I knew that between us there are ties that make us one; now open that door, or tell me that the girl we seek is not here.

TOM. [*with axe*] Then see for yourselves. [*He breaks doors open. Annie as a boy comes down*] It's only my little brother Phil from Omaha.

FOR ENCORE.

TOM. Yes ma-am, little Phil come hyar to his brother's wedding, praps it will only be a funeral after all; please ma-am give him shelter for to-night.

CORI. Neely take the boy to the Ranch.

JOE. Where a den is Annie Smalley?

TOM. Away from the murderous hand of bad men and human devils; off on the path of duty, with her woman's wit and the grit of a lioness, seekin for proofs agin the man who murdered the Indian gal.

JOE. Dat is you.

TOM. No you! robber, coward, cut-throat!

JOE. Prove it!

ROB. Tell him you will.

TOM. I take your challenge man, and with the help of strong hands and brave hearts, I will prove it.

CURTAIN.

TABLEAUX I.

SCENE.—*Corrall as before. Enter JOE and gang with rope which they throw across limb of tree. He knocks at door. TOM comes out.*

TOM. What do you want hyar, pardners?

JOE. Al McClelland you kill dat a gal Silver Bud—dat not enough, oh no! you find Annie Smalley, make much talk at trial in Cheyene; you get her here and kill all same as Silver Bud; where is dat a grave you make? Come, tell quick!

TOM. You unclean lot of half starved wolves, get out of this hyar place, it is mine!

JOE. The only part of dat place you own is dare.　[*points to rope suspended*]

TOM. What you devils!　[*Terrible struggle, Tom finally gets a brand from the fire and puts it behind door.*　Look hyar you half breed Coyotees, do you think I will ever let my neck go inside of that noose?　[*Terrible struggle*]　Stop! you fiends of perdition, save your strength and breath to say your prayers, for in another moment, I will send you out over the prairie like rotten chips.　Help!

Terrible explosion, everything falls, discovering the Ranch in flames.　ANNIE *at window screaming.*　TOM *rushes in, climbs to roof, breaks in and bears Annie from the burning house.*

CURTAIN.

TABLEAUX II.

SCENE III.—*Rocky Mountain Pass, bridge down and masked in with snow rocks, snow wings, snow falling, wind howling, mountain drop in 4.　Calcium ready.* AL *discovered on rock down centre in rags covered with blood.　Moon shines out.*

AL. Alone on these awful heights, falling from cliff to chasm: broken in body and in spirit, and reason tottering on its throne and yet he must be near me now, Tom! will you let me die here alone in the ice and snow, alone on the Peak?　[*falls on rock.*

ANNIE *and* SCRIPTURE *appear at back and cross.*

SCRIPT. Come my poor child it is useless, you had better return to the camp, or you will perish with hunger and cold.

ANNIE. No, Parson, he was seen passing Wild Cry Gulch: have we not followed his bloody tracks in the snow?　I have toiled to find him as never woman toiled before: and I will find him, dead or alive; I *will* find him!　[*They Exit.　Storm again.*

Enter ANNIE *and* SCIPTURE. *Moonlight, she discovers Al.*

ANNIE. I have found him, Parson! thank heaven. I have found him.

AL. Who is there?

ANNIE. Annie. Al, your own Annie; don't you know me darling?

AL. (*faintly*) Yes, yes.

ANNIE. Come to nurse you back to life; come from the Ranch and from Tom who is there.

AL. Tom at the Ranch, is he well?

ANNIE. Yes he is [*looks at Parson*] well.

AL. Thank heaven.

ANNIE. Ranch 10 has been destroyed by fire; Tom saved me from the flames; he has been taken for you and imprisoned for the murder of Silver Bud. Oh Al! arouse yourself; you and I will return to right this terrible wrong, or bear with Tom our share of this great misfortune.

AL. [*with effort*] I'll go now Annie. [*falls back*] who is with you Annie?

ANNIE. A good brave clergyman, Tom's friend who has been with me during all this weary journey.

AL. Quick! Parson; this girl, make her my wife. [*Business*

PARSON. Do you take this man to be your lawful wedded husband?

ANNIE. I do.

PARSON. Do you take this woman to be your lawful. wedded wife?

AL. I do.

PARSON. Then I pronounce you man and wife; those whom God has joined together; let no man put assunder.

AL. [*Faintly. Falling*] Amen! Annie—going fast—glad of it—pain awful. Tell brother Tom, that both of us must live again in him. Tell him to love you as I have loved, and to do by you as I would have done; it don't matter which can claim you Annie, we will be altogether; Al, Tom, Annie and little Phil from Omaha.   [*Dies*]

ANNIE. Dead, and by a murderer's hand! the blood on the prairie grass, and in the snow, alike call aloud for vengeance!

PARSON. The avenger of blood is your God.

ANNIE. And I am his child; guided by his hand, and strenghened by his love, I devote my life to placing in the power of justice, the man who committed this double murder.

PARSON. A righteous cause.

ANNIE. Heaven deal with me, as I attempt this holy duty.

CURTAIN.

ACT III.

SCENE IV.—*Interior of Court Room in Cheyenne, W.T. Judge on elevated seat. Jury in their places, Spectators crowded at back. JOE in their midst. CORI. and NEELY seated. Several gentlemen seated at table, C. writing. ROBBINS in the rear of table.*

JUDGE PROSE. In opening this Court it becomes my duty, I may say my pleasure, gentlemen, to disparage the sloth and lack of punctuality on the part of the officers of this august and deliberate body; on the other hand I compliment the jury on the promtness they evince in being in their places, even before the head of the court has taken his seat; the absence of the other officers must be looked into, and if guilty of neglect, they shall be punished; it is reprehensible, inadmissable, inexcusable, actionable, culpable.

ROB. [*breaking in*] Damnable.

JUDGE. Who said that? If I knew I would commit him instantly. Where is the prisoner? Where are the Court Officers?

ROB. The prisoner will be here at once; I answer for him.

JUDGE. Who are you, sir?

ROB. Deputy in charge of the prisoner.

JUDGE. I have heard that he is out on bail; a first degree murder case on bail; who is his bail?

ROB. I am; since Ranch No. 10 was destroyed, he has been living at Stemmer's Ranch, forty miles north of No. 10; he pledged his word to appear on time for trial, and I allowed him the freedom of the Territory.

JUDGE. Most extraordinary, arbitrary, elocutionary, and inobligatory; you have no right in the premises, sir. I'll consult the authorities, sir. [*turns over books*] it is unprecedented, immaterial, unconstitutional; who is his counsel?

ROB. At the prisoner's request, I shall act for him.

JUDGE. You! don't you think you'd better run the Court yourself; I shall consult the authorities, sir; as for the other officers—where are they? Where's the Prosecuting Attorney?

ROB. He was shot last night.

JUDGE. What! how dare he! it's a direct insult to this august body; is he too sick to appear?

ROB. No, he's dead.

JUDGE. Dead ! then he's excused; Clerk of the Court send me a live lawer.

ROB. The Clerk was lynched at daylight this morning.

JUDGE. What for?

ROB. For shooting the Prosecuting Attorney.

JUDGE. Excuse him also.

ROB. Thanks your Honor, we'll try to.

JUDGE. Don't be so dogmatical, sir, so unpoetical, so emphatical; Lawyer Holt we select you to represent the government and prosecute the prisoner.

HOLT. [*rising from table*) This is very sudden, your Honor: no time for preparation.

JUDGE. Time ! what more time do you want—you've got a whole hour; not a word, sir, or I'll commit you. Sheriff Robbins, go into that Billiard Room opposite, and tell my son David to come over here and act as Clerk of this august body.

ROB. Yes, your Honor, decisively, immediately, instantaneously.

JUDGE. Go, sir !

ROB. Spasmodically. [*Exit up* C. *door*]

JUDGE. While we are waiting, we might as well go ahead; the witnesses—where are they ? I'll make sure of them at least. [*reads from paper*] Joseph Kebook.

JOE. [*springs up shouting*] Here a your Honor !

JUDGE. Well you are alive at all events.   Coriander L. Smalley.

CORI. [*rising*] Well, what do you want with me ?

JUDGE. Answer to your name.

CORI. You know my name.

JUDGE. Say, here !

CORI. Where ?

JUDGE. (*shouting*) There !

CORI. Oh, here.

JUDGE Why could'nt you say here at first ?   Neely Barrett.

NEELY. Good morning, sir.

JUDGE. Answer to your name.

NEELY. How did you know my name ?

JUDGE. Say here !

NEELY. Sure I aint there.

JUDGE. [*shouting*] Say here !

NEELY. Of course I hear, ye spake loud enough. [*goes up.*

Enter ROBBINS.

JUDGE. Well Sheriff, did you find my son David, and order him to come here and act as Clerk ?

ROB. I told him.

JUDGE. What did he say ?

ROB. He said he'd see you hung first.

JUDGE. [*Flustering*] What ! what ! how dare you talk about hanging in court ! what else did he say ?

ROB. He said one crank in the family was enough.

JUDGE. The graceless whelp, I'll commit him.

ROB. I told him so.

JUDGE. What did he say ?

ROB. He said if you did you'd die with your boots on.

JUDGE. Ahem ! ahem ! excuse him also; where shall I get a clerk ?

ROB. I will act as Clerk.

JUDGE. You will soon fill every office in the commonwealth; it's unhallowed, invalid; I'll consult the authorities.

ROB. Judge, I am the most versatile man in Wyoming Territory; I'll serve as Clerk.

JUDGE. It's not altogether in accordance with the authorities, but we'll try it. [*He administers oath to Robbins*] Where's the prisoner, sir ?

ROB. [*Looks at watch. Aside*] He's an hour behind time.

JOE. [*From the crowd*] He will not a come.

JUDGE. Who says that ? Come here ! [*Joe comes down*]

ROB. Your Honor, this man is the active enemy of the absent prisoner; if he does not come, I forfeit what I have deposited. Who's most entitled to respect and belief? This ruffian who bullies women, and who has been spit on by every cow-boy in the Territory, or I, a man, a medical authority, a scientist and a politcal.

JUDGE. You take advantage of your position, sir.

ROB. What position, for heavens sake !

JUDGE. Every position in this Court, sir, except that of judge ! and I aint at all sure you wont grab that before the trial's over. [*to Joe*] Now speak man, what do you know ?

JOE. I know dat jury indict him for a murder, and den he

out on bail; I know that as soon as we all left Stemmer's Ranch, McClelland watch a close, jump on a pony and a start for Downer's where he can take a train East; same time I make a miss big pile of money, $5,000; you find dat money on him I bet, when we make a catch him.

CORI. That's a matter of opinion ! Judge I don't believe this amphibious Bushwacker; he swore my niece Annie Smalley was in the Corrall with McClelland; we caught him in that lie, and now he lies again; I answer for it, on the reputation of a woman, a bondholder and an old maid.

JUDGE. But where is he ? I'll consult the authorities.

CORI. [*crosses to Rob*] Doctor, this begins to look bad; what with Annie's disappearance, the murder, the Ranche's destruction, and now Al McClelland's running away, I'm quite broke up.

ROB. Hush ! I can't believe ill of him; I have perfect confidence in his word.

JUDGE. Start in pursuit at once ! shoot him wherever found !

ROB. Judge give us a little time.

JUDGE. Not a moment ! his release is most extraordinary unexplanatory, uncomplimentary; I order you to collect a posse of men and start for Downer's, shoot him if he makes the least resistance.

JOE. I a volunteer a go.

JUDGE. Start at once, this Court is dissolved. [*all rise. Cheers outside.*

ROB. [*runs to door.*] I was right, the noble fellow on his horse, tearing over those garden patches—over they go ! down ! he is killed ! no, it's the horse ! up again; look at him run ! three cheers for Al McClelland ! [*all cheer, he rushes on.*]

TOM. Robbins I killed the pony, but I've saved the saddle and bridle. Gentleman I will explain all; this yhar man tried to bribe me to forsake my pledged word, and run away from them that has befriended me; he fearing to face this Court and the almighty truth, he hoped to follow me up, shoot me in the dark and recover this hyar wallet marked with his name, and loaded with 5,000 dirty dollars; thus branding me in the moment of death, a thief as well as a murderer and perjured villian; Red Bullet when you left me out thar on the prairie, you left a devil in my heart, and this pile of money in my hand

you told me Annie Smalley was at Downer's waiting to fly with
me to the east; I saw freedom all around me, and death hyar.
what did I do—I turned my heart inside out, kicked the devil
black and blue, stabbed my spurs into Robbin's horse, and
am hyar to hand you back your bundle of green temptation.
with a clear conscience and a warm soul.

HOLT. (*Reading*) [*written*] *We, the members of the Grand
Jury convened according to Law, to hear and decide upon such
criminal case as may be presented to us, do hereby render a true
Bill of Indictment against Albert McClelland for the murder of an
Indian Woman, known as Silver Bud, on the 3rd day of September,
1871, and believing according to our oaths that the evidence against
the said McClelland is of such weight that he should be tried before
a Judge and Jury, it is so ordered.*

(*Signed*) William Hardy,

Foreman Jury.

JUDGE. Prisoner you have heard the idictment, what say you
are you guilty or not guilty?

TOM. Not guilty, so help me heaven !

JUDGE. You must never mention heaven in the Court, it's in-
discreet, uncircumspect, indirect. Go on sir.

HOLT. Gentleman of the jury, the prosecution has been
allowed but little time for research and deliberation, but I find
upon examination of the evidence given before the Grand Jury,
the case against the prisoner is so firmly establised, that I shall
not be obliged to trouble you with a lengthy preamble; I will
show you from the testimony of reliable witnesses, first, that
there existed a strong motive for this murder; I will show you
that the woman Silver Bud, held relations with the prisoner not
in accordance with law or morality.

TOM. You'r wrong thar pardner.

JUDGE. Sit down or I'll commit you.

TOM. I thought I was pretty well committed already, Pardner.

ROB. Keep cool.

TOM. I will man if I kin.

HOLT. The jury can draw their own conclusions from these
interruptions; I say his motive in wishing to be rid of the deceased was that he might marry a young heiress, named Annie
Smalley. I will show you that just before the shot was fired,

McClelland was engaged in an angry controversy with the deceased, that the accused was found terror stricken by the body his double barrel shot gun with one barrel discharged, smoking by his side. In short, gentleman, I intend to show so clearly the guilt of this unfortunate man, that you will render a verdict for the people without leaving your seats. Call Joseph Kebook.

Rob. Joseph Kebook. [*He rushes into box*] No need to call him, he's in the box already. [*Rob. takes bible from Judge's Stand and administers oath*]

Holt. What is your name?

Joe. Joseph a Kebook.

Holt. Were you a witness to the quarrel that took place between the prisoner and the deceased just before the murder? If so, tell the jury what you heard.

Judge. Remember you are on your oath.

Rob. Much he cares about that.

Joe. I was a come over dat a prairie to dat hotel call No. 10, and a heard a noise, loud noise, much make fight with a mouth, I a wait and listen.

Rob. Then you were spying about the place, were you?

Joe. No, hiss!

Judge. Order!

Rob. I have a right to question.

Judge. No sir, not by the authorities, if you are drawing four salaries at one time.

Holt. Go on Mr. Kebook.

Joe. Moon be bright, I saw Al and Bud, she make a loud howl and cry, and he say damn, hiss, like de debil; putty soon her make a run back a putty good a way, raise his gun and make a fire; Silver Bud fall, putty quick I guess.

Holt. Very well, was it generally known that the accused bore questionable relations with the deceased?

Rob. (*springing up*) I object most emphatically, dogmatically and bald headedly!

Judge. We overrule your objection.

Rob. I tell you Judge you are stroking the cat the wrong way.

Judge. I'll consult the authorities.

Holt. Answer, was this known?

Joe. It was known by every cow-boy inside a fifty mile.

HOLT. That will do Mr. Kebook.

ROB. No it wont do Mr. Kebook! stay right where you are, [*Joe hangs his head*] take your eyes off your big feet and look at me; when I am talking with a man I like to see the whites of his eyes; did the prisoner at the bar ever knock you down with a Billard Cue in Brady's Saloon for cheating at Poker?

JOE. Me no make a cheat.

ROB. Look up you whimpering calf, did he knock you under the table—answer!

JOE. Yes—hiss!

ROB. You love him very much, don't you, hey? Look up answer!

JOE. No, hate! damn! hiss!

ROB. You did not hate the girl Silver Bud, did you, hey?

JOE. No, nice a gal.

ROB. Did you not woo her, and try to induce her to live with you; be careful, McClelland got the best and stole the girl's heart? Speak!

JOE. (*angry*) Yes! hate, hiss! he make a steal.

ROB. I thought so, he beat you with a Billiard Cue and then captured your sweetheart—what other name are you known by than Kebook?

JOE. (*grins proudly*) Red a Bullet: because I make a bullet out of copper—copper he red.

ROB. Tell the jury what the Red Bullet is like.

JOE. Long a like my finger, he make a big hole when he strike.

ROB. You know copper is a poison?

JOE. Yes, sure kill.

ROB. (*takes out the Bullet he picked up in the first act*) Is that a genuine Red Bullet?

HOLT. I object to this! what has it to do with the case?

ROB. I wish to show the jury what kind of a man Mr. Kebook is, he confesses he murders men with copper poison.

JUDGE. Answer the question, is it yours?

JOE. (*looks at it*) Yes, a mine sure.

ROB. (*hands it to Foreman*) Look at it gentleman, a nice weapon truly. get out of sight. (*shakes hands with Tom*) First knock down for our side.

JUDGE. You musn't talk about knocking down, it's against the authorities.

ROB. Oh, the authorities be——

JUDGE. Stop sir ! don't you damn the authorities.

ROB. I didn't damn them.

JUDGE. You came damned near it.

HOLT. Is this a Court of Justice or a beer dive ?

JUDGE. Keep Silence and call the witnesses !

HOLT. Coriander L. Smalley.

ROBBINS *writes note and sends it.*   CORI. *gets into box, and is given Bible, which the Judge hands to Rob.*

CORI. What's this ?

ROB. The Holy Bible.

CORI. "Read and Return." Union Pacific Rail Road Co., why this was stole off the Chicago cars, (*to Judge*) Oh, you old scamp !

JUDGE. It aint my bible woman ! swear her.

ROB. I must swear you.

CORI. I don't want to swear.

JUDGE. Why not ?

CORI. Because I'm a Quaker.

JUDGE. A whater ?

CORI. A Quaker.

JUDGE. What's a Quaker ?

CORI. Consult the authorities.

HOLT. This scene would disgrace a lynch trial.

JUDGE. Sit down ! I fine you ten dollars,

HOLT. You'll have to charge it then.

ROB. Take the oath Miss Smalley. [*oath administered*]

HOLT. What is your name ?

CORI. Coriander Lucretia Smalley; I run Ranch No. 10; am a sour old maid, and I'm glad of it.

HOLT. Do you know the prisoner at the Bar ?

CORI. Where's the Bar? I don't see any Bar.

JUDGE. Not a drinking Bar, woman ! a Bar of Justice.

CORI. Where's the Justice ?

JUDGE. I'm the Justice.

CORI. Where's your Bar ?

JUDGE. (*furious*) I tell you I hav'nt any Bar, woman !

CORI. [*points to his nose*] You ought to get that sign painted out then.

JUDGE. I fine you ten dollars !

CORI. It's worth twenty.

HOLT. Do you know the prisoner ?

CORI. Yes.

HOLT. Tell the jury what you know about the case in question.

CORI. (*weakening a little*) I—I— I was startled from my kitchen about nine o'clock, where I was making stew for breakfast, (*turns to Neely*) wasn't it stew Neely ?

NEELY. No ma-am it was tripe.

JUDGE. Never mind the tripe.

CORI. I went out on the porch, I saw two people on the ground, I went down to them, and I—I—I knew he didn't do it (*bursts into tears.*)

HOLT. No tears please, go on.

JUDGE. Hold on ! does 'em good; let her cry.

HOLT. Will your Honor inform me if this is a pool room or a Court of Justice ?

JUDGE. You'd better be careful, sir.

HOLT. I'll be careful, go on Miss smalley, whom did you find the persons on the ground to be ?

CORI. Silver Bud and Al McClelland; she was dead and he was bending over her.

HOLT. Did you hear any quarrel previous to hearing the shot fired ?

CORI. Yes, they—they—were having loud words.

HOLT. Was the gun near by ?

CORI. Yes—one—one barrel was empty, some of the men blew into it, smoke came out.

HOLT. What do you know of the relations existing between the deceased and McClelland ?

JUDGE. Hold on ! I may be an old crank, but I've got a wife and daughter myself, and I'd shoot any man who would ask them such a question; she need not answer if she don't want to in spite of all the authorities from Blackstone to Chicago.

HOLT. That's sufficient, her silence is more eloquent to the jury than her speech; stand down Miss Smalley.

ROB. Hold on ! how long have you known the accused ?

CORI. Since he was a ten-pound calf of a baby; he and his brother Tom.

ROB. His character?

CORI. A generous big hearted donkey.

JUDGE. But he blew up your premises, and destroyed your home.

CORI. He did it to save himself from a lot of sneaking cow-punchers; as for the Ranch, it was tolerably well insured.

JUDGE. Didn't lose much, hey?

CORI. There's a heap of snow on the ground, and the thermometer away below zero when one of the Smalley family misses the train.

ROB. Be serious, is he a man likely to have murdered a poor girl who loved him?

CORI. He would rather have put the muzzle of that gun under his chin and blown his own head off, than have harmed a finger nail of that poor dead Indian.

TOM. Thanks ma-am, here's looking towards you.

ROB. [*Takes up a double-barred shot gun and hands it to her.*] Will you be good enough to look at this; can you identify it?

CORI. Yes, it belonged to McClelland; we found it on the ground near the body.

ROB. Thanks ma-am, stand down.

HOLT. Neely Barrett.

ROB. Neely Barrett!

NEELY. [*gets into box*] Oh, I hear you! do you expect me to fly like a Crow or a Sea-gull? (ROBBINS *holds out Bible*) Now Doctor dear I'll take my oath, I can't swear.

JUDGE. Why not, why not?

NEELY. Because I'm another Quaker.

ROB. Take the book like a good girl. (*she takes it.   Oath administered*) Judge, dear.

JUDGE. Kiss the book and swear.

NEELY. All right, I'll kiss the book, but I wont swear. [*She kisses it.*]

HOLT. What is your name?

NEELY. (*not noticing him*) It's the first time I ever heard of swearing and kissing going together.

HOLT. Your name, I say!

NEELY. You don't say, Miss Barrett.

HOLT. Your full name!

NEELY. I was never full in my life, ye blaguard!

HOLT.. Both your names?

NEELY. It's Neely Barrett now; when I get married it will be something else.

JUDGE. Heaven help the man!

NEELY. Who knows but it might be your Honor there!

JUDGE. I fine you ten dollars.

NEELY., Have you change for a twenty?

JUDGE. This is too much even for a Cheyenne jury to stand; *now stop* and *go on.*

HOLT. Miss Barrett, do you know the prisoner, Al McClelland?

NEELY. I do; I'd like to kiss him, poor fellow.'

TOM. Here's looking towards you, Miss.

HOLT. Tell the jury everything you know regarding the murder of Silver Bud.

NEELY. Well, then after leaving the kitchen and hearing the gun go off, I came out; Silver Bud poor little thing—she and I used to sleep in the one bed— when I came out, there was the poor little toad lying on the ground. and Mr. Al there, a crying and a praying and praying; oh! it was as good as a mass to hear him.

HOLT. Where was the gun?

NEELY. Some of the men had it, blowing into the little key-hole to see if it was shot off.

HOLT. Was it empty or full?

NEELY. (*Hesitating*) Well—well, I—one of the triggers was empty, and the other was full.

HOLT. Well?

NEELY. Then they took poor Al away to the constable, as if he had been a buffalo, and then (*weeps*) I took poor little Bud in my arms, wid her purty brown face close up to me, and I said, Bud ye poor little gossom, are ye dead; but not a whisper did she speak, and that's the last word I ever heard from her lips.

HOLT. That will do.

ROB. Stop! Miss Barrett.

NEELY. I will Doctor dear, make me say something good about him.

ROB. How long have you known the prisoner?

Neely. (*hesitates*) Well, well. in—in three years more, I'll have known him four years.

Rob. Is his character good ?

Neely. Yes sir, better than good. it's the boss.

Rob. One word more, do you think the disappearance of your young mistress. Miss Smalley, is to be attributed to him ?

Neely. No sir; they would both of them died to save the other. There ! that's my opinion of him, and now not another bit of kissing and swearing do you get from between my lips.

[*goes to seat.*]

Holt. Annie Smalley. [*Rob. whispers to Holt.*] Strange, if she had nothing to tell against her lover. why is she not here ?

Rob. (*aside to Tom*) Man if you have any word to explain away this mystery. say it now.

Tom. (*after a struggle*) I have nothing to say, pardner.

Joe. But I have a got !

Holt. Get in the box.

Joe. I know dat Miss Smalley went to dat Corrall before I call up people in Ranch No. 10: we break open gate, no one in-side. door of shed locked; den door broke open.

Holt. What did you find ?

Joe. Only nudder boy. he say. Phil from Omaha, his budder.

Rob. This is entirely irrelevant, we are wasting time.

Holt. I wish to show that the prisoner was instrumental in removing this dangerous witness.

Judge. Allowed. go on.

Holt. What became of Annie Smalley?

Joe. She killed by dem two budders and buried somewhere in dat Corrall. den he blow up dat Ranch to hide his crime, and say he do it to save him from de lynch. bah ! lie ! hate ! hiss !

[*Tom makes a spring for him. Rob holds him.*

Tom. Can that thar nasty greaser live ?

Rob. Hush, man. be patient !

Cori. Let Kebook go on, I begin to see it all now— I have been blind.

Tom. Oh, Miss Smalley ! how kin you ? (*aside*) Friend after friend is leaving me. and I dare not speak a word.

Cori. She went in there, I am sure now has never been seen since.

Rob. She may have perished in the flames.

CORI. No, she was not in the Ranch when it was burnt. [*Tom seizes Robbins and drags him down centre.*

TOM. (*in frenzy*) Robbins, man! I must tell all or I shall go clean mad.

ROB. Speak out then, Al McClelland!

TOM. Robbins—I—I—I am not—

ROB. What?

TOM. (*with a mighty effort*) I——I am, not guilty, that's all. [*they go up*] Judge, jury, enemies, *friends*, if I have one hyar. I stand hyar a forsaken creature accused of awful crimes; proof after proofs are flung against me; in return, I kin only hit back by saying I am innocent.

JUDGE. I have heard a hundred murderers say the same.

TOM. True: I am lost unless she should come back. (*aside*) It is too late to speak now, if I would. Judge she must come, she is not dead.

Enter ANNIE veiled.

JOE. Yes she is dead.

TOM. Thank heaven! (*pulls off veil*) she—is—not—dead. [*She runs into Tom's arms: Neely and Cori. embrace her. He takes her down*) Annie, sweet little yankee violet, have you come a last!

ANNIE. (*sobbing*) Yes, Tom.

HOLT. I protest! this endearing scene is simply introduced to melt the jury.

JUDGE. Shut up! you are a married man yourself perhaps. if you aint, I'd advise you to catch on at once. This Court will now adjourn for five consecutive minutes. [*they go off*]

ANNIE. Listen: from this time forth you are to be Al McClelland in reality, just as you now assume the name.

TOM. Al?—Speak out Annie, what of my brother?

ANNIE. Dead! (*he chokes*) O, don't, I am weak you must be strong.

ANNIE. Your friend, Parson Jim Scripture from Idaho. joined me in the search for Al, who had been seen in the vicinity of your claim; when we reached the mountains a great storm was in progress, we found Al dying with hunger and cold:— his last words were love for you; tell Tom said he, that when I am dead, both of us must live again in him. I want him to do by you and love you as I would have done; and you Annie do the same by him: in death we will not be parted, said he, I will be with you, it don't matter which of us may claim you; then the darkness came and the cruel cutting blizzard; when the light again appeared, my husband lay frozen in my arms.

Tom. Your husband?

Annie. Wife and widow.

Tom. Hold up your head Annie, let us be worthy of the brave man who died down thar in Colorado. [*they go up*]

Judge. Now then, if your little family affairs are starched and ironed, we will begin the more serious work of the day. [*with dignity*] Attention! order! silence! I mean it this time.

Holt. Annie Smalley.

Annie. (*gently*) Here, sir. [*goes in box, is sworn*]

Holt. Do you know the prisoner at the Bar?

Annie. Yes sir.

Holt. A conscientious witness— were you at Ranch 10 on the night of Silver Bud's murder?

Annie. Yes sir.

Holt. A most conscientious witness— be kind enough to throw aside all personal feeling and tell the jury all you know regarding the murder.

Annie. There was the report of a gun, we rushed from the house; Silver Bud lay dead; McClelland was leaning over the body, his hands bloody, his gun discharged.

Holt. Here's evidence enough to hang a saint.

Rob. Confine yourself to the witness, and no side speeches to the jury.

Holt. My case is strong enough without doing so— go on Miss Smalley, you are a most conscientious witness; what more?

Annie. Every appearance of guilt, and yet he is as innocent as I am.

Holt. What do you mean?

Tom. (*immitating him*) Pardner, she means she is a most con-scientious witness.

Holt. You are speaking as lover, not as a witness.

Annie. No sir. I am speaking to you as a truthful woman, who is confident in the right, and who is here to speak her con-victions.

Holt. This is mere clap trap, and woman's nonsense.

Tom. Pardner, she is a most conscientious witness.

HOLT. I demand that you proceed!

JUDGE. Hold on let me get in a word: the lady has said quite enough in the interest of justice; Miss Smalley, if you don't want to give irrelevant evidence in my court against the man you love, you shant be compelled to do it, no sir ree! not if it breaks the bank. Robbins, I am sorry to send the case to the jury in this shape, but I must if you have no one to summon for the defense.

ROB. One moment sir, we are ready for the defense. Judge, it may not be in accordance with law or precedent, but like a good fellow, have to-day shown yourself superior to both; take this book and swear me, and let me tell my story, and this brave girl's story to these men who have it on their lips to say guilty of murder in the first degree.

HOLT. I suppose it's no use for me to offer an objection.

JUDGE. Not a bit— Robbins I'm your man though I may be hung myself for this days work. [*Oath administered*]

ROB. For a very limited time, Miss Annie Smalley has been the guest of a quiet family in Cheyenne; to whose care, at her request I confided her, with what object you shall yourselves judge. I delayed the following explanation until her arrival, and until the policy of the prosecution was fully defined; now I am ready to speak. On the night of the murder of Silver Bud, this agonized woman stood over the body, looked into the gentle face and made up her mind that no such man as Al McClelland ever put out that little light; yet there was all the evidence and nothing but her loving trust in his manhood to cling to.

The remains were buried near the Ranch, and Al McClelland held for the crime; now see what followed; acting upon her subtile suggestion, I last night disentered that body and made an examination of the same. Our little heroine there, holding the flickering lantern, her face averted, her limbs trembling, but at every throb of her brave heart whispering, go on; I proceeded to explore the wound; I found the entrance on the right side, the missile having passed across the chest, struck a rib near the heart and there lost its power; the projectile remaining fixed in the rib. Now hear, if ever you heard in your lives, Al McClelland did not murder that woman! how do I know? Listen, the cause of her death was not a charge of shot, but a bullet! and they don't fire bullets out of double barrel shot guns.　　　[*Joe

moves silently to door] Hold on Joe, don't go away appearing
slighted; come here and let me see the whites of your eye.

JOE. (*comes down*) What do you a want of me? Hiss!

ROB. I want to tell a you a little stolly—hiss! I tried to
draw the bullet from the rib, but the bone was so firmly fixed
about the metal, that it was immovable; now see what I did:
I took my little saw, and I cut that little rib out of that little
body; the rib was Silver Bud's, and the projectile fastened in it
was a genuine red bullet, the personal property of Joseph Kebook, the man who killed her first, and then traduced her good
name! [*holds up bullet and rib*] See the rib and the bullet!
Examine it gentleman, and see how it compares with the other
[*gives it to Jury.*]

JUDGE. Miss Smalley, is this evidence in accordance with the
truth?

ANNIE. In every particular.

TOM. He owned the same to me in the Corrall at Ranch 10.

ROB. From that mad confession we got our first clue.

JUDGE. Do you wish to sum up for the prosecution, Mr Holt?
[*Holt rises, takes his bag and walks deliberately out of the door.*]
Consult the authorities. The jury will now retire and not return until they have agreed upon a verdict: that is the only
charge I have to give you.

FOREMAN. We have agreed your honor.

JUDGE. Do you find the prisoner at the bar guilty or not
guilty.

FOREMAN. Not guilty.

JUDGE. Discharge Mr. McClelland, and arrest Kebook on a
bench warrant. (*Jury all go off and wait for Joe.*)

ROB. Here Joe, you are invited to assimulate with yonder
jovial assembly: leave your gun.

JOE. (*goes to door*) I have a Jive without a dam fear, I will
a die without a dam fear, with a my a boots on!

JUDGE. From present appearances, I think you will, unless
you pull 'em off inside of five minutes.

JOE. Me no fear dem, no fear you; damn! hate! hiss! *Exit.*

JUDGE. I am afraid the law majestic will never get a whack
at Mr. Joe Kebook.

CORI. Al McClelland in reward for your suffering and manly
straight backedness, I'm going to give that girl into your keep- •

ing for life; Judge make 'em man and wife on the spot, and I will give you a hundred dollars.

TOM. Do you hear—his last words, do you accept?

ANNIE. In the name of his love, I do.

TOM. The hand of Fate!

ANNIE. No, the hand of Heaven.

TOM. As he would have done by you, so I will do, when it is for your good, sis.

JUDGE. [*down*] McClelland, I came here expecting to sentence you to death; the law decides to punish you in another way: imprisonment for life; your jailer will now take you in charge. Madame do you approve the sentence?

CORI. That's a matter of opinion.

ROB. Miss Coriander, I will never have a better impulse than that which now makes my heart jump; I am fifty, you ten years my junior; make me your prisoner and let us all go to jail together.

CORI. (*holds out hand*) That's not a matter of opinion.

JUDGE. Is Mr. Albert McClelland ready for the ceremony, and will——

TOM. (*tenderly*) Stop! pardner, Al McClelland will never be ready.

ROB. What!

CORI. How dare you?

TOM. (*mos' tenderly*) Bear with me please, a moment, until I kin git the hold of my own speech—such a marriage would not be lawful, and for all time to come, thar must be only flowers and heaven's sun for this tired one hyar. [*Annie clings to him.*

CORI. Speak! man.

TOM. Thar were created two brothers, so exact alike in face and form that when thar came a deal for life and death between the two, thar war only one who could say out of her swelling heart, this hyar is the man I love and this, his brother.

One of these twins, Al, war accused of an awful crime; his brother Tom jumped between him and sartin death; Al fled and died on the wild peaks of Colorado seeking his brother; Tom stayed, war tried for the murder, war saved by heaven and this yhar dear girl.

CORI. [*crosses c.*] You are!

TOM. A rough fellar who loves her jist as strong as did Al

McClelland, but who will let the poor tired one rest until perhaps, some day her smile may come back, and her eyes may brighten up into mine, and then I'll be iron sure that Al's word has become her wish and she'll be the wife of Tom McClelland from Colorado.

CURTAIN.